To Imani, to all my Faith.
—I. X. K.

To all the young people, whose own imaginations are unbound by
the imaginations of state violence and white supremacy, and the power
we hold to build a world that is Antiracist. I believe in us.
—A. L.

KOKILA
An imprint of Penguin Random House LLC, New York

First published in the United States of America by Kokila,
an imprint of Penguin Random House LLC, 2020

Text copyright © 2020 by Ibram X. Kendi
Illustrations copyright © 2020 by Ashley Lukashevsky

Library of Congress Cataloging-in-Publication Data is available.

Printed in the United States of America

10 9 8 7 6 5 4
ISBN 9780593110508

Design by Jasmin Rubero • Text set in Aniara Regular with Gill Sans Regular

We would like to acknowledge the contribution of the educators from #DisruptTexts
(Tricia Ebarvia, Lorena Germán, Kim Parker, and Julia E. Torres) in collaborating on the
discussion questions for parents and caregivers.

To review a full discussion guide by #DisruptTexts visit bit.ly/AntiracistBabyGuide

ANTIRACIST BABY

ILLUSTRATIONS BY

IBRAM X. KENDI   ASHLEY LUKASHEVSKY

Kokila

Antiracist Baby is bred, *not* born.

Antiracist Baby is raised
to make society transform.

Babies are taught to be racist or antiracist—there's no neutrality.

Take these nine steps to make equity a reality.

1 Open your eyes to all skin colors.

Antiracist Baby learns all the colors,
not because race is true.
If you claim to be color-blind,
you deny what's right in front of you.

2 Use your words to talk about race.

No one will see racism if we only stay silent.
If we don't name racism,
it won't stop being so violent.

3 Point at policies as the problem, not people.

Some people get more, while others get less . . .
because policies don't always grant equal access.

4 Shout, "There's nothing wrong with the people!"

Even though all races are not treated the same,

"We are all human!" Antiracist Baby can proclaim.

Antiracist Baby doesn't see certain groups as "better" or "worse." Antiracist Baby loves a world that's truly diverse.

6 Knock down the stack of cultural blocks.

Antiracist Baby appreciates how groups speak, dance, and create as they choose. Antiracist Baby welcomes all groups voicing their unique views.

7 Confess when being racist.

Nothing disrupts racism more than when we confess
the racist ideas that we sometimes express.

8 Grow to be an antiracist.

Antiracist Baby is always learning, changing, and growing.

Antiracist Baby stays curious about all people and isn't all-knowing.

Antiracist Baby is filled with
the power to transcend, my friend.
And doesn't judge a book by its cover,
but reads until . . .

THE END.

Dear Parents and Caregivers,

It is critical that we begin explicit conversations about race and racism with our children from a young age. Just as we teach our kids to be kind even before they fully understand what it means to be kind, we should teach our kids to be antiracist even before they fully understand what it means to be antiracist. When we are afraid to talk about race, kids assume that it's a topic that they, too, are supposed to avoid. Since studies show that children are exposed to racist messages all around them in our society, it is our responsibility to counter those messages by helping children learn to be antiracist.

Here are some questions and discussion starters to encourage conversations about race and racism with young children.

Ask your child: "When you imagine a farmer, a teacher, or an astronaut—what do they look like?"

You might find that kids default to white authority figures in their imaginations. Ask them about why this might be so. This could lead to conversations about how we must be conscientious and critical of the images we're presented in media. What is the effect of setting the default for authority figures to white?

Ask your child to describe the people in their friend group and yours.

It is a fallacy that children are "color-blind." Help your child explicitly name the race of the people around them so they understand it is not insulting or harmful to do so. We want to normalize discussions about race and remove the stigma around these conversations.

It is important for children to name the race of the people around them so you can ask them what they think about those different races, why they think those things, and instruct them on how to understand racial difference—as an imagined construct, but one with very real consequences. You want to teach them this. You don't want to assume children are "blank slates"—this leaves room for racist societal messages to shape their understanding of racism instead.

Help children understand that racist policies are the problem, not people.

You and the child can reflect on the racial makeup of your school or neighborhood. Are they truly diverse? Or do you live in a neighborhood or attend a school that is segregated? Help children understand that this is a result of racist policy, and talk about how this affects which schools may receive more resources over others. Or discuss how children who experience poverty, food insecurity, or homelessness are disproportionately Black and brown. Ask the child why they think this may be the case and talk about the conditions that caused this, making clear it is not the fault of the Black or brown child or their parents.

Challenge the idea that all people are treated the same.

It is common to share lessons like "be kind to everyone" with kids, but this reinforces the idea that racist acts are only carried out on an individual level and ignores that all people are not given the same access to necessary resources. Although we might teach kids that "anyone can do anything," we also have to teach them that racist barriers exist that stop us all from being truly free. Understanding this is the first step in helping to change it. Being kind does not mean that we avoid seeing race, but that we celebrate racial differences.

Share your own experiences with racism.

The heartbeat of racism is denial. If you can model for a child that it is okay to confess our own racist beliefs and actions and how we are working to change them, they are less likely to be ashamed when we point out how they may have absorbed a message from society that is truly racist.

For example, if a child expresses that they think darker-skinned people are less beautiful than lighter-skinned people, you can perhaps share a time when you thought so, how and why you changed, and what you now know—that all of the skin colors are equally beautiful. Engage kids in discussion about how messaging in the stories, advertisements, and toys they see might have given

them this idea so they can recognize it, reject it, and form a new understanding without being held back by shame or embarrassment.

Remember to talk to your kids about how people aren't just "racist" or "antiracist," but rather how their actions can be racist or antiracist.

Kids might understand how this is similar to when we say we don't consider them to be "a bad kid" when they do something wrong, but we must acknowledge that they made a bad choice. They have the opportunity to make a better choice the next time, because we know that identity is not fixed. Being antiracist is about what we do, not who we are. Being measured by our actions allows us to continue to grow.

-Ibram X. Kendi